MADAGASCAR™

MAD LIBS®

By Roger Price and Leonard Stern

PSS!
PRICE STERN SLOAN

DreamWorks
ANIMATION SKG

PRICE STERN SLOAN
Published by the Penguin Group
Penguin Group (USA) Inc., 375 Hudson Street, New York, New York 10014, USA
Penguin Group (Canada), 10 Alcorn Avenue, Toronto, Ontario, Canada M4V 3B2
(a division of Pearson Penguin Canada Inc.)
Penguin Books Ltd, 80 Strand, London WC2R 0RL, England
Penguin Ireland, 25 St Stephen's Green, Dublin 2, Ireland (a division of Penguin Books Ltd)
Penguin Group (Australia), 250 Camberwell Road, Camberwell, Victoria 3124, Australia
(a division of Pearson Australia Group Pty Ltd)
Penguin Books India Pvt Ltd, 11 Community Centre, Panchsheel Park,
New Delhi-110 017, India
Penguin Group (NZ), Cnr Airborne and Rosedale Roads,
Albany, Auckland 1310, New Zealand (a division of Pearson New Zealand Ltd)
Penguin Books (South Africa) (Pty) Ltd, 24 Sturdee Avenue,
Rosebank, Johannesburg 2196, South Africa

Penguin Books Ltd, Registered Offices: 80 Strand, London WC2R 0RL, England

Mad Libs format copyright © 2005 by Price Stern Sloan

Madagascar TM & © 2005 DreamWorks Animation L.L.C.
All rights reserved.

Published by Price Stern Sloan,
a division of Penguin Young Readers Group,
345 Hudson Street, New York, New York 10014.

Printed in the United States of America. No part of this publication may be reproduced, stored
in any retrieval system, or transmitted, in any form or by any means, electronic, mechanical,
photocopying, or otherwise, without the prior written permission of the publisher.

ISBN 0-8431-1588-2

1 3 5 7 9 10 8 6 4 2

PSS! and *MAD LIBS* are registered trademarks of Penguin Group (USA) Inc.

MAD LIBS®
INSTRUCTIONS

MAD LIBS® is a game for people who don't like games! It can be played by one, two, three, four, or forty.

• RIDICULOUSLY SIMPLE DIRECTIONS

In this tablet you will find stories containing blank spaces where words are left out. One player, the READER, selects one of these stories. The READER does not tell anyone what the story is about. Instead, he/she asks the other players, the WRITERS, to give him/her words. These words are used to fill in the blank spaces in the story.

• TO PLAY

The READER asks each WRITER in turn to call out a word—an adjective or a noun or whatever the space calls for—and uses them to fill in the blank spaces in the story. The result is a MAD LIBS® game.

When the READER then reads the completed MAD LIBS® game to the other players, they will discover that they have written a story that is fantastic, screamingly funny, shocking, silly, crazy, or just plain dumb—depending upon which words each WRITER called out.

• EXAMPLE (*Before* and *After*)

"_____!" he said _____
       EXCLAMATION   ADVERB

as he jumped into his convertible _____ and
                                   NOUN

drove off with his _____ wife.
                    ADJECTIVE

"*Ouch!*_____!" he said *stupidly*_____
   EXCLAMATION   ADVERB

as he jumped into his convertible *cat*_____ and
                               NOUN

drove off with his *brave*_____ wife.
                ADJECTIVE

MAD LIBS
QUICK REVIEW

In case you have forgotten what adjectives, adverbs, nouns, and verbs are, here is a quick review:

An ADJECTIVE describes something or somebody. *Lumpy, soft, ugly, messy,* and *short* are adjectives.

An ADVERB tells how something is done. It modifies a verb and usually ends in "ly." *Modestly, stupidly, greedily,* and *carefully* are adverbs.

A NOUN is the name of a person, place, or thing. *Sidewalk, umbrella, bridle, bathtub,* and *nose* are nouns.

A VERB is an action word. *Run, pitch, jump,* and *swim* are verbs. Put the verbs in past tense if the directions say PAST TENSE. *Ran, pitched, jumped,* and *swam* are verbs in the past tense.

When we ask for A PLACE, we mean any sort of place: a country or city *(Spain, Cleveland)* or a room *(bathroom, kitchen).*

An EXCLAMATION or SILLY WORD is any sort of funny sound, gasp, grunt, or outcry, like *Wow!, Ouch!, Whomp!, Ick!,* and *Gadzooks!*

When we ask for specific words, like a NUMBER, a COLOR, an ANIMAL, or a PART OF THE BODY, we mean a word that is one of those things, like *seven, blue, horse,* or *head*.

When we ask for a PLURAL, it means more than one. For example, *cat* pluralized is *cats*.

MAD LIBS® is fun to play with friends, but you can also play it by yourself! To begin with, DO NOT look at the story on the page below. Fill in the blanks on this page with the words called for. Then, using the words you have selected, fill in the blank spaces in the story.

Now you've created your own hilarious MAD LIBS® game!

THE NEW YORK GIANTS

ADJECTIVE_____

ADJECTIVE_____

A PLACE _____

VERB ENDING IN "ING" _____

TYPE OF SPORT _____

NOUN _____

ADJECTIVE_____

NOUN _____

PLURAL NOUN _____

TYPE OF FOOD (PLURAL) _____

VERB _____

VERB ENDING IN "ING" _____

PLURAL NOUN _____

ADJECTIVE_____

ADJECTIVE_____

ADJECTIVE_____

MAD LIBS
PENGUINS POP-UP

After Marty finished another _____ performance for
                                    ADJECTIVE

the _____ crowd in the zoo, he returned to his
        ADJECTIVE

_____ pen and sat quietly. He was still thinking
   ADJECTIVE

about how he was going to get to _____. Suddenly,
                                    FOREIGN COUNTRY

four penguin _____ popped out of the ground in
              PART OF THE BODY (PLURAL)

Marty's pen. He was _____ surprised and yelled,
                            ADVERB

"_____!" The penguins told him that they
   EXCLAMATION

were planning on _____ all the way to
                    VERB ENDING IN "ING"

_____! Since Marty also wanted to go there,
  FOREIGN COUNTRY

they talked about a/an _____ escape. Marty wished
                              ADJECTIVE

he had a/an _____ so he could go on the Internet and
                NOUN

find the most _____ way to get there, but the
                  ADJECTIVE

penguins had their own _____ plans. They
                              ADJECTIVE

had bought _____ and were planning to
              PLURAL NOUN

_____ there!
      VERB

From MADAGASCAR MAD LIBS®, Madagascar TM & © 2005 DreamWorks Animation L.L.C. Published by Price Stern Sloan, a division of Penguin Young Readers Group, 345 Hudson Street, New York, New York 10014.

MAD LIBS® is fun to play with friends, but you can also play it by yourself! To begin with, DO NOT look at the story on the page below. Fill in the blanks on this page with the words called for. Then, using the words you have selected, fill in the blank spaces in the story.

Now you've created your own hilarious MAD LIBS® game!

AN APPLE A DAY *DOESN'T* KEEP THE DOCTOR AWAY

NOUN _____

NOUN _____

CELEBRITY (MALE) _____

NOUN _____

ADJECTIVE _____

NOUN _____

ADJECTIVE _____

PLURAL NOUN _____

NOUN _____

VERB _____

NUMBER _____

PLURAL NOUN _____

VERB _____

NOUN _____

VERB ENDING IN "ING" _____

MAD LIBS
AN APPLE A DAY *DOESN'T* KEEP THE DOCTOR AWAY

Poor Melman! He always has a cold or a sore _____.
                                                 NOUN

In order to avoid blowing his _____ all day long, he
                                  NOUN

follows orders from his doctor, _____. Here's what
                                 CELEBRITY (MALE)

you can do to stay healthy, too:

1. Drink a large glass of _____ juice first thing in the
                              NOUN

morning. It's full of _____ vitamins.
                         ADJECTIVE

2. Take a multi-_____ every day. They contain
                    NOUN

_____ minerals like calcium and _____.
 ADJECTIVE   PLURAL NOUN

3. Whenever you feel a/an _____ coming on, you
                              NOUN

must get lots of rest. Make sure you _____ for at
                                         VERB

least _____ hours and wear warm _____.
       NUMBER   PLURAL NOUN

4. If you start to _____, immediately eat a/an
                      VERB

_____. It will stop you from _____.
   NOUN   VERB ENDING IN "ING"

From MADAGASCAR MAD LIBS®, Madagascar TM & © 2005 DreamWorks Animation L.L.C. Published by Price Stern Sloan, a division of Penguin Young Readers Group, 345 Hudson Street, New York, New York 10014.

MAD LIBS® is fun to play with friends, but you can also play it by yourself! To begin with, DO NOT look at the story on the page below. Fill in the blanks on this page with the words called for. Then, using the words you have selected, fill in the blank spaces in the story.

Now you've created your own hilarious MAD LIBS® game!

A GREAT ESCAPE

ADJECTIVE_____

ADJECTIVE_____

FOREIGN COUNTRY _____

VERB (PAST TENSE)_____

NOUN _____

ADJECTIVE_____

SILLY WORD_____

VERB (PAST TENSE)_____

ADJECTIVE_____

SAME FOREIGN COUNTRY_____

NOUN _____

OCCUPATION _____

ADJECTIVE_____

NOUN _____

EXCLAMATION_____

MAD LIBS
A GREAT ESCAPE

Marty was worried about leaving the _____ zoo
                                        ADJECTIVE

and all his _____ friends, but he really wanted to see
              ADJECTIVE

what life was like in _____. So late one night, he
                        FOREIGN COUNTRY

_____ his way out of the huge _____ that the
VERB (PAST TENSE)   NOUN

penguins built for him and made his _____
                                         ADJECTIVE

escape! He was so excited, he yelled _____ and
                                        SILLY WORD

_____ over the front gate of the zoo. Since he needed
VERB (PAST TENSE)

a/an _____ ticket to get to _____, he
       ADJECTIVE   SAME FOREIGN COUNTRY

headed straight for Grand Central _____. Luckily, he
                                       NOUN

spotted a/an _____ horse who knew the way. The
               OCCUPATION

horse got Marty there safe and _____! Marty was so
                                   ADJECTIVE

grateful that he gave the horse a huge _____.
                                             NOUN

"_____!" the surprised horse replied.
  EXCLAMATION

From MADAGASCAR MAD LIBS®, Madagascar TM & © 2005 DreamWorks Animation L.L.C. Published by Price Stern Sloan, a division of Penguin Young Readers Group, 345 Hudson Street, New York, New York 10014.

MAD LIBS® is fun to play with friends, but you can also play it by yourself! To begin with, DO NOT look at the story on the page below. Fill in the blanks on this page with the words called for. Then, using the words you have selected, fill in the blank spaces in the story.

Now you've created your own hilarious MAD LIBS® game!

ODE TO STEAK

NOUN _____

ADJECTIVE_____

ADJECTIVE_____

NOUN _____

NOUN _____

VERB ENDING IN "ING" _____

NOUN _____

ADJECTIVE_____

VERB _____

VERB ENDING IN "ING" _____

ADJECTIVE_____

VERB _____

ADJECTIVE_____

MAD LIBS
ODE TO STEAK

While Alex waited in his _____ for his _____ steak
                          NOUN   ADJECTIVE
to arrive, he wrote a/an _____ poem about his very
                            ADJECTIVE
favorite _____. Here's what he wrote:
            NOUN

Any way you slice it

_____ is my most favorite food.
   NOUN

When _____ on my _____,
     VERB ENDING IN "ING"   NOUN

It puts me in a/an _____ mood.
                     ADJECTIVE

Steak is my favorite, yes it is.

I _____ it every day.
     VERB

I love it _____ on my plate,
          VERB ENDING IN "ING"

Especially in a sauté.

So _____ steak, I give you praise.
     ADJECTIVE

What more is there to say?

I love to _____ you day and night,
              VERB

On a/an _____ silver tray.
           ADJECTIVE

From MADAGASCAR MAD LIBS®, Madagascar TM & © 2005 DreamWorks Animation L.L.C. Published by Price Stern Sloan, a division of Penguin Young Readers Group, 345 Hudson Street, New York, New York 10014.

MAD LIBS® is fun to play with friends, but you can also play it by yourself! To begin with, DO NOT look at the story on the page below. Fill in the blanks on this page with the words called for. Then, using the words you have selected, fill in the blank spaces in the story.

Now you've created your own hilarious MAD LIBS® game!

SUBWAY DOS AND DON'TS

VERB ENDING IN "ING" _____

NOUN _____

NOUN _____

VERB _____

NUMBER _____

PLURAL NOUN _____

PLURAL NOUN _____

CELEBRITY (FEMALE) _____

VERB ENDING IN "ING" _____

NOUN _____

PLURAL NOUN _____

PLURAL NOUN _____

ADJECTIVE _____

PLURAL NOUN _____

PLURAL NOUN _____

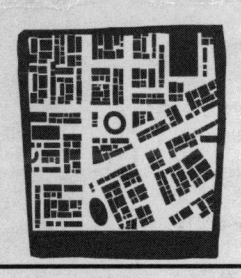

MAD LIBS
SUBWAY DOS AND DON'TS

Here are some tips for _____ on a New York
                                VERB ENDING IN "ING"

subway _____.
              NOUN

1. Make sure to buy a/an _____ before you
                                      NOUN

_____ through the turnstile. It only costs
        VERB

_____ dollars.
    NUMBER

2. There are lots of great _____ who play their
                                    PLURAL NOUN

_____ for money in subway stations. Last
    PLURAL NOUN

week the famous singer _____ was spotted
                              CELEBRITY (FEMALE)

_____ her _____ !
  VERB ENDING IN "ING"   NOUN

3. If you need to use the bathroom, don't put the _____
                                                        PLURAL NOUN

in your mouth. They are really _____ used to clean
                                      PLURAL NOUN

the toilets!

4. On the train, keep away from the _____ doors.
                                            ADJECTIVE

5. Leave the special _____ open for senior
                            PLURAL NOUN

_____.
    PLURAL NOUN

From MADAGASCAR MAD LIBS®, Madagascar TM & © 2005 DreamWorks Animation L.L.C. Published by Price Stern Sloan, a division of Penguin Young Readers Group, 345 Hudson Street, New York, New York 10014.

MAD LIBS® is fun to play with friends, but you can also play it by yourself! To begin with, DO NOT look at the story on the page below. Fill in the blanks on this page with the words called for. Then, using the words you have selected, fill in the blank spaces in the story.

Now you've created your own hilarious MAD LIBS® game!

I LOVE NEW YORK

NOUN _____

ADJECTIVE_____

VERB _____

ADJECTIVE_____

PLURAL NOUN _____

CELEBRITY (FEMALE) _____

TYPE OF FOOD (PLURAL) _____

VEHICLE _____

NOUN _____

VERB ENDING IN "ING" _____

NOUN _____

VERB (PAST TENSE)_____

NOUN _____

NOUN _____

NOUN _____

NOUN _____

NOUN _____

ADJECTIVE_____

CELEBRITY (MALE)_____

MAD LIBS
I LOVE NEW YORK

After Marty's escape from the zoo, he couldn't wait to explore the big _____ ! There were so many _____ things
         NOUN   ADJECTIVE
to do! The first was _____ on a subway and head to Times
                           VERB
Square. It was a/an _____ experience filled with bright
                          ADJECTIVE
_____ , tons of people, and even _____
  PLURAL NOUN   CELEBRITY (FEMALE)
selling _____ from a/an _____ !
        TYPE OF FOOD (PLURAL)   VEHICLE
Next, Marty headed to Rockefeller _____ . He couldn't
                                          NOUN
wait to go ice _____ in the _____ rink!
               VERB ENDING IN "ING"   NOUN
Then he _____ on a double-decker _____
         VERB (PAST TENSE)   NOUN
and went to the top of the Empire _____ Building. He
                                          NOUN
could see the entire city by looking through a/an _____ .
                                                        NOUN
Finally he went to Broadway to see a musical _____ ,
                                                    NOUN
The _____ of the Opera, which he thought was pretty
      NOUN
_____ . Afterward he waited outside and got an
   ADJECTIVE
autograph from _____ . What an adventure!
                 CELEBRITY (MALE)

From MADAGASCAR MAD LIBS®, Madagascar TM & © 2005 DreamWorks Animation L.L.C. Published by Price Stern Sloan, a division of Penguin Young Readers Group, 345 Hudson Street, New York, New York 10014.

MAD LIBS® is fun to play with friends, but you can also play it by yourself! To begin with, DO NOT look at the story on the page below. Fill in the blanks on this page with the words called for. Then, using the words you have selected, fill in the blank spaces in the story.

Now you've created your own hilarious MAD LIBS® game!

UNDER ARREST

ADVERB _____

SILLY WORD _____

NOUN _____

CITY _____

ADJECTIVE _____

PLURAL NOUN _____

PART OF THE BODY (PLURAL) _____

PART OF THE BODY _____

VERB (PAST TENSE) _____

PLURAL NOUN _____

PLURAL NOUN _____

PLURAL NOUN _____

PLURAL NOUN _____

NOUN _____

MAD LIBS
UNDER ARREST

Alex, Gloria, and Melman **quickly** (ADVERB) ran after Marty through Grand Central **ginuinu** (SILLY WORD). They didn't want him getting on a/an **pizza** (NOUN) and going to **New York** (CITY). Gloria ran up the **fast** (ADJECTIVE) escalator to try to catch Marty. But since Melman was wearing **bikes** (PLURAL NOUN) on his hands and **eardrums** (PART OF THE BODY (PLURAL)), he couldn't run fast enough! By the time Gloria and Melman arrived, Alex had caught up to Marty and was pinning him down and sitting on his **skull** (PART OF THE BODY). As the gang grabbed Marty and **skied** (VERB (PAST TENSE)) back to the zoo, they ran into a large group of **football players** (PLURAL NOUN) and policemen. As the Zoosters tried to run away, the policemen shot darts filled with **Papa Johns** (PLURAL NOUN) into their **yoga mats** (PLURAL NOUN), and the animals fell asleep. When they woke up, they were in giant **aqua raiders** (PLURAL NOUN) on a slow-moving **lightbulb** (NOUN).

From MADAGASCAR MAD LIBS®, Madagascar TM & © 2005 DreamWorks Animation L.L.C. Published by Price Stern Sloan, a division of Penguin Young Readers Group, 345 Hudson Street, New York, New York 10014.

MAD LIBS® is fun to play with friends, but you can also play it by yourself! To begin with, DO NOT look at the story on the page below. Fill in the blanks on this page with the words called for. Then, using the words you have selected, fill in the blank spaces in the story.

Now you've created your own hilarious MAD LIBS® game!

MISSION IMPOSSIBLE

ADJECTIVE_____

FOREIGN COUNTRY _____

NOUN _____

VERB _____

SILLY WORD_____

CELEBRITY (MALE)_____

VERB ENDING IN "ING" _____

VEHICLE _____

FOREIGN COUNTRY _____

PART OF THE BODY _____

SAME VEHICLE_____

ADVERB_____

EXCLAMATION_____

PLURAL NOUN _____

MAD LIBS
MISSION IMPOSSIBLE

The penguins were on a/an _____ boat on its way to
                              ADJECTIVE

_____, and they wanted to escape. Luckily, Rico had
FOREIGN COUNTRY

saved a/an _____ and was able to _____
              NOUN   VERB

the lock open on their crate! They were so excited, they yelled

_____! Then they snuck into the control room
 SILLY WORD

and found the captain listening to _____ on the
                                      CELEBRITY (MALE)

stereo and _____ loudly. This was the perfect chance
            VERB ENDING IN "ING"

to take over the _____ and get to _____!
                    VEHICLE   FOREIGN COUNTRY

Kowalski gave the captain a karate chop to his _____
                                                PART OF THE BODY

that knocked him to the ground. The penguins grabbed the wheel

of the _____ and _____ turned it around.
        SAME VEHICLE   ADVERB

_____! At a speed of ten _____ per hour,
 EXCLAMATION   PLURAL NOUN

they would arrive at their destination in no time.

From MADAGASCAR MAD LIBS®, Madagascar TM & © 2005 DreamWorks Animation L.L.C. Published by Price Stern Sloan, a division of Penguin Young Readers Group, 345 Hudson Street, New York, New York 10014.

MAD LIBS® is fun to play with friends, but you can also play it by yourself! To begin with, DO NOT look at the story on the page below. Fill in the blanks on this page with the words called for. Then, using the words you have selected, fill in the blank spaces in the story.

Now you've created your own hilarious MAD LIBS® game!

CASA DEL WILD

ADJECTIVE_____

PLURAL NOUN _____

PLURAL NOUN _____

ADJECTIVE_____

ADJECTIVE_____

VERB _____

PLURAL NOUN _____

A PLACE _____

ADJECTIVE_____

PLURAL NOUN _____

TYPE OF FOOD (PLURAL) _____

PLURAL NOUN _____

PLURAL NOUN _____

ADJECTIVE_____

SOMETHING ALIVE (PLURAL) _____

PLURAL NOUN _____

MAD LIBS
CASA DEL WILD

When he arrived in Madagascar, Marty decided to build himself a/an

_____ new home. First, he gathered _____
    ADJECTIVE   PLURAL NOUN

from the beach to build the framework for his house. He used a

hammer, _____, and a screwdriver to make sure his
              PLURAL NOUN

home would be very _____. He poured _____
                            ADJECTIVE   ADJECTIVE

cement to _____ up the holes and then constructed
                  VERB

the front door out of _____. Then he took a trip to the
                            PLURAL NOUN

_____ to get some _____ items for
   A PLACE   ADJECTIVE

decorating. He found fluffy _____, a new grill to roast
                              PLURAL NOUN

_____, and some candles that smelled just like
TYPE OF FOOD (PLURAL)

_____. In his living room, he placed a couch made out
 PLURAL NOUN

of _____ and some _____ pillows. He
   PLURAL NOUN   ADJECTIVE

got some fresh _____ to put in vases and
                  SOMETHING ALIVE (PLURAL)

hung curtains from the top of the _____.
                                         PLURAL NOUN

From MADAGASCAR MAD LIBS®, Madagascar TM & © 2005 DreamWorks Animation L.L.C. Published by Price Stern Sloan, a division of Penguin Young Readers Group, 345 Hudson Street, New York, New York 10014.

MAD LIBS® is fun to play with friends, but you can also play it by yourself! To begin with, DO NOT look at the story on the page below. Fill in the blanks on this page with the words called for. Then, using the words you have selected, fill in the blank spaces in the story.

Now you've created your own hilarious MAD LIBS® game!

KING JULIEN

PLURAL NOUN _____

ADJECTIVE_____

ADJECTIVE_____

NOUN _____

NOUN _____

VERB _____

VERB _____

ADJECTIVE_____

SILLY WORD_____

ADJECTIVE_____

TYPE OF FOOD (PLURAL) _____

VERB _____

CELEBRITY (FEMALE) _____

CELEBRITY (MALE) _____

ADJECTIVE_____

NOUN _____

NOUN _____

NOUN _____

ADJECTIVE_____

NOUN _____

MAD LIBS
KING JULIEN

Welcome, ladies and _____. I am King Julien,
                            PLURAL NOUN

the _____ leader of the lemurs on this
      ADJECTIVE

_____ island. Isn't this a beautiful _____?
ADJECTIVE   NOUN

Let me show you around. To the left we have a/an _____,
                                                                NOUN

where all of the lemurs meet to _____ and
                                              VERB

_____. On the right we have the lemurs'
     VERB

_____ hangout, the _____, where we
ADJECTIVE   SILLY WORD

have our _____ parties. We eat _____,
             ADJECTIVE   TYPE OF FOOD (PLURAL)

_____ to the latest tunes from _____
    VERB   CELEBRITY (FEMALE)

and _____, and have a really _____ time.
      CELEBRITY (MALE)   ADJECTIVE

But the best part of this island is that I am the king! I get to live in

a giant _____, eat gourmet _____,
         NOUN   NOUN

and sleep in a king-sized _____. All of the
                                        NOUN

_____ lemurs must listen to every word I say because I
ADJECTIVE

am the _____.
         NOUN

From MADAGASCAR MAD LIBS®, Madagascar TM & © 2005 DreamWorks Animation L.L.C. Published by Price Stern Sloan, a division of Penguin Young Readers Group, 345 Hudson Street, New York, New York 10014.

MAD LIBS® is fun to play with friends, but you can also play it by yourself! To begin with, DO NOT look at the story on the page below. Fill in the blanks on this page with the words called for. Then, using the words you have selected, fill in the blank spaces in the story.

Now you've created your own hilarious MAD LIBS® game!

LOCAL LEMURS

ADJECTIVE_____

PLURAL NOUN _____

COLOR_____

PLURAL NOUN _____

PLURAL NOUN _____

PLURAL NOUN _____

NUMBER _____

ANIMAL (PLURAL) _____

PLURAL NOUN _____

ADJECTIVE_____

PLURAL NOUN _____

ADJECTIVE_____

VERB ENDING IN "ING" _____

ADJECTIVE_____

COLOR_____

NOUN _____

PLURAL NOUN _____

CELEBRITY (MALE)_____

MAD LIBS
LOCAL LEMURS

The _____ lemurs of Madagascar are the cutest
           ADJECTIVE
_____ that you will ever meet. They have fuzzy
 PLURAL NOUN
_____ _____, tiny _____,
  COLOR   PLURAL NOUN   PLURAL NOUN
and great big _____. They have lived on the island
                PLURAL NOUN
for over _____ years and are actually the ancestors of
          NUMBER
_____. They live in small _____ and
 ANIMAL (PLURAL)   PLURAL NOUN
sleep in _____ beds made out of _____.
           ADJECTIVE   PLURAL NOUN
Their favorite hobbies are watching _____ movies
                                         ADJECTIVE
and going to _____ events. Although the lemurs
              VERB ENDING IN "ING"
are really _____, no one is cuter than Mort. With
             ADJECTIVE
his big _____ _____ and bright white
          COLOR   NOUN
_____, he looks just like _____!
    PLURAL NOUN   CELEBRITY (MALE)

From MADAGASCAR MAD LIBS®, Madagascar TM & © 2005 DreamWorks Animation L.L.C. Published by Price
Stern Sloan, a division of Penguin Young Readers Group, 345 Hudson Street, New York, New York 10014.

MAD LIBS® is fun to play with friends, but you can also play it by yourself! To begin with, DO NOT look at the story on the page below. Fill in the blanks on this page with the words called for. Then, using the words you have selected, fill in the blank spaces in the story.

Now you've created your own hilarious MAD LIBS® game!

FOSSAS

ADJECTIVE _____

VERB _____

PLURAL NOUN _____

NUMBER _____

PART OF THE BODY (PLURAL) _____

PERSON IN ROOM (MALE) _____

PART OF THE BODY (PLURAL) _____

ADJECTIVE _____

PLURAL NOUN _____

VERB _____

ADJECTIVE _____

VERB ENDING IN "ING" _____

EXCLAMATION _____

NOUN _____

VERB ENDING IN "ING" _____

NUMBER _____

CELEBRITY (MALE) _____

FOREIGN COUNTRY _____

MAD LIBS
FOSSAS

Beware! We are the _____ fossas of Madagascar. When
                       ADJECTIVE
you see us approaching, _____ for your life! We are
                              VERB
the most ferocious _____ ever created. We weigh
                      PLURAL NOUN
_____ pounds, have huge _____,
   NUMBER   PART OF THE BODY (PLURAL)
and look just like _____. With our sharp
                      PERSON IN ROOM (MALE)
_____, our _____ claws, and long
 PART OF THE BODY (PLURAL)   ADJECTIVE
bushy _____, we will _____ anyone that comes
       PLURAL NOUN   VERB
our way, especially the lemurs. They are so _____.
                                                ADJECTIVE
Whenever they see us _____ toward them, they
                       VERB ENDING IN "ING"
yell "_____!" and run to the _____. We
      EXCLAMATION   NOUN
have been _____ the residents of Madagascar for
            VERB ENDING IN "ING"
_____ years. That's longer than _____ has
   NUMBER   CELEBRITY (MALE)
been king of _____!
              FOREIGN COUNTRY

From MADAGASCAR MAD LIBS®, Madagascar TM & © 2005 DreamWorks Animation L.L.C. Published by Price Stern Sloan, a division of Penguin Young Readers Group, 345 Hudson Street, New York, New York 10014.

MAD LIBS® is fun to play with friends, but you can also play it by yourself! To begin with, DO NOT look at the story on the page below. Fill in the blanks on this page with the words called for. Then, using the words you have selected, fill in the blank spaces in the story.

Now you've created your own hilarious MAD LIBS® game!

DAY IN THE LIFE OF MORT

NOUN _____

NOUN _____

VERB _____

PLURAL NOUN _____

NOUN _____

VERB _____

ADJECTIVE_____

TYPE OF FOOD_____

TYPE OF FOOD (PLURAL) _____

PLURAL NOUN _____

VERB _____

ADJECTIVE_____

COLOR_____

CELEBRITY (MALE)_____

MAD LIBS
DAY IN THE LIFE OF MORT

It's not easy being me! Although I try to be the best _____
NOUN
I can be, none of the other lemurs seem to like me that much.
Even though I kiss King Julien's _____, I still get in trouble.
NOUN
And I think the fossas are trying to _____ me! Last
VERB
week they tied my _____ and threw me into a
PLURAL NOUN
giant wooden _____! Luckily I managed to
NOUN
_____, but it wasn't easy! And just when I thought
VERB
I was _____, King Julien and the other lemurs
ADJECTIVE
wanted to sacrifice me to Alex, who thought I was a piece of
_____. After I managed to escape, King
TYPE OF FOOD
Julien stuffed me with _____, wrapped me in
TYPE OF FOOD (PLURAL)
_____, and tried to get Gloria to _____
PLURAL NOUN   VERB
me. It's just not fair. I mean, I can't help that I have the most
_____ _____ eyes of all the lemurs, can
ADJECTIVE   COLOR
I? And it's not my fault that I look just like _____!
CELEBRITY (MALE)

From MADAGASCAR MAD LIBS®, Madagascar TM & © 2005 DreamWorks Animation L.L.C. Published by Price Stern Sloan, a division of Penguin Young Readers Group, 345 Hudson Street, New York, New York 10014.

MAD LIBS® is fun to play with friends, but you can also play it by yourself! To begin with, DO NOT look at the story on the page below. Fill in the blanks on this page with the words called for. Then, using the words you have selected, fill in the blank spaces in the story.

Now you've created your own hilarious MAD LIBS® game!

LEMURS' PARTY PLANNING GUIDE

ADJECTIVE_____

ADJECTIVE_____

PLURAL NOUN _____

ADJECTIVE_____

ADJECTIVE_____

PLURAL NOUN _____

CELEBRITY (MALE)_____

LAST NAME OF PERSON IN ROOM_____

ADJECTIVE_____

NOUN _____

NOUN _____

ADJECTIVE_____

NOUN _____

TYPE OF FOOD (PLURAL) _____

MAD LIBS
LEMURS' PARTY PLANNING GUIDE

The lemurs really know how to throw the most
_____ parties! Follow their tips and you can have
    ADJECTIVE

your own _____ bash!
           ADJECTIVE

1. Remember to wear your very best _____.
                                             PLURAL NOUN

2. You should always have a/an _____ selection of
                                    ADJECTIVE

music. Make sure to have a/an _____ assortment of
                                        ADJECTIVE

_____ to suit everyone's tastes. _____
 PLURAL NOUN   CELEBRITY (MALE)

and Jessica _____ are always good choices.
          LAST NAME OF PERSON IN ROOM

3. When sending out your _____ invitations, be sure
                                 ADJECTIVE

to have everyone's correct mailing _____. Last time
                                        NOUN

the lemurs threw a party, Mort's invitation got lost in the

_____.
  NOUN

4. Always be sure to serve a wide selection of _____
                                                                   ADJECTIVE

food for your guests. I recommend _____ cheese and
                                                  NOUN

_____.
TYPE OF FOOD (PLURAL)

From MADAGASCAR MAD LIBS®, Madagascar TM & © 2005 DreamWorks Animation L.L.C. Published by Price Stern Sloan, a division of Penguin Young Readers Group, 345 Hudson Street, New York, New York 10014.

MAD LIBS® is fun to play with friends, but you can also play it by yourself! To begin with, DO NOT look at the story on the page below. Fill in the blanks on this page with the words called for. Then, using the words you have selected, fill in the blank spaces in the story.

Now you've created your own hilarious MAD LIBS® game!

COME TO ORDER!

PLURAL NOUN _____

NOUN _____

NOUN _____

PLURAL NOUN _____

VERB (PAST TENSE) _____

ADJECTIVE _____

ADJECTIVE _____

ADJECTIVE _____

NOUN _____

NOUN _____

NOUN _____

PLURAL NOUN _____

ADJECTIVE _____

MAD LIBS
COME TO ORDER!

King Julien and the _____ were worried about how
                     PLURAL NOUN
to deal with the New Yorkers. They met one night high up in a/an

_____, where a giant _____ had
      NOUN   NOUN
crashed, so they could discuss their plan of action. "Now, lemurs,

what should we do about our guests, the New York

_____?" asked King Julien. The lemurs _____
 PLURAL NOUN   VERB (PAST TENSE)
and agreed that they all really liked the _____ zoo
                                              ADJECTIVE
animals, especially since they kept them safe from the

_____ fossas. King Julien decided that they would
    ADJECTIVE
become friends with their new visitors and make the Zoosters as

_____ as possible in their new _____.
    ADJECTIVE   NOUN
When the Zoosters awoke the next morning, the _____
                                                      NOUN
had been transformed into a tropical _____, filled
                                            NOUN
with exotic _____ and _____ trees!
              PLURAL NOUN   ADJECTIVE

From MADAGASCAR MAD LIBS®, Madagascar TM & © 2005 DreamWorks Animation L.L.C. Published by Price Stern Sloan, a division of Penguin Young Readers Group, 345 Hudson Street, New York, New York 10014.

MAD LIBS® is fun to play with friends, but you can also play it by yourself! To begin with, DO NOT look at the story on the page below. Fill in the blanks on this page with the words called for. Then, using the words you have selected, fill in the blank spaces in the story.

Now you've created your own hilarious MAD LIBS® game!

AT THE WATERING HOLE

NOUN _____

ADJECTIVE _____

PART OF THE BODY (PLURAL) _____

ADVERB _____

PLURAL NOUN _____

SILLY WORD _____

ADJECTIVE _____

VERB (PAST TENSE) _____

ADJECTIVE _____

PART OF THE BODY (PLURAL) _____

PLURAL NOUN _____

TYPE OF FOOD _____

VERB _____

VERB _____

ADJECTIVE _____

SILLY WORD _____

MAD LIBS
AT THE WATERING HOLE

The lemurs gathered in the _____ to watch a/an
                                    NOUN

_____ performance by the zoo animals. They couldn't
   ADJECTIVE

believe their _____! Alex started to yell
              PART OF THE BODY (PLURAL)

_____, flashed his pearly white _____,
    ADVERB   PLURAL NOUN

and let out a huge _____. Then he started doing
                      SILLY WORD

push-ups for the _____ crowd. The lemurs
                         ADJECTIVE

_____ wildly! Things got really _____. Alex
 VERB (PAST TENSE)   ADJECTIVE

threw his _____ into the air, and his sharp
          PART OF THE BODY (PLURAL)

_____ came out. Then he started seeing things! As he
 PLURAL NOUN

looked at the lemurs, he imagined that they were really juicy pieces

of _____. As he started to _____,
   TYPE OF FOOD   VERB

he grabbed his best friend Marty and tried to _____
                                                  VERB

him! The lemurs were so _____ that they called Alex
                            ADJECTIVE

a/an _____ and banished him to the fossas' side of the
     SILLY WORD

island.

From MADAGASCAR MAD LIBS®, Madagascar TM & © 2005 DreamWorks Animation L.L.C. Published by Price Stern Sloan, a division of Penguin Young Readers Group, 345 Hudson Street, New York, New York 10014.

MAD LIBS® is fun to play with friends, but you can also play it by yourself! To begin with, DO NOT look at the story on the page below. Fill in the blanks on this page with the words called for. Then, using the words you have selected, fill in the blank spaces in the story.

Now you've created your own hilarious MAD LIBS® game!

A SLICE OF ADVICE

CELEBRITY (FEMALE) _____

ADJECTIVE_____

NOUN _____

VERB ENDING IN "ING" _____

ADJECTIVE_____

TYPE OF FOOD _____

ADVERB_____

NOUN _____

VERB ENDING IN "ING" _____

PLURAL NOUN _____

SILLY WORD_____

ADJECTIVE_____

SAME CELEBRITY (FEMALE)_____

ADJECTIVE_____

ADJECTIVE_____

MAD LIBS
A SLICE OF ADVICE

Dear _____,
      CELEBRITY (FEMALE)

I can't believe that I tried to hit my _____ friend
                                              ADJECTIVE

Marty on the _____. I really didn't mean to do it, but
               NOUN

_____ here in Madagascar has made me do some
VERB ENDING IN "ING"

_____ things. And I can't stop thinking about
ADJECTIVE

enjoying a big, juicy _____. What should I do?
                         TYPE OF FOOD

Even though I apologized to Marty and told him how

_____ I feel, the lemurs still made me leave my
ADVERB

_____ and live with the fossas. I miss my friends so
NOUN

much that I feel like _____ out loud. I can't help
                VERB ENDING IN "ING"

being a lion. Even though I have sharp _____
                                           PLURAL NOUN

and a loud roar that sounds like _____, I am really
                                  SILLY WORD

_____ on the inside. Please, _____, give
ADJECTIVE   SAME CELEBRITY (FEMALE)

me some _____ advice.
          ADJECTIVE

A Very _____ Lion,
        ADJECTIVE

Alex

From MADAGASCAR MAD LIBS®, Madagascar TM & © 2005 DreamWorks Animation L.L.C. Published by Price Stern Sloan, a division of Penguin Young Readers Group, 345 Hudson Street, New York, New York 10014.

MAD LIBS® is fun to play with friends, but you can also play it by yourself! To begin with, DO NOT look at the story on the page below. Fill in the blanks on this page with the words called for. Then, using the words you have selected, fill in the blank spaces in the story.

Now you've created your own hilarious MAD LIBS® game!

TIME TO CELEBRATE!

NOUN _____

SOMETHING ALIVE (PLURAL) _____

ADJECTIVE_____

ADJECTIVE_____

VERB _____

PART OF THE BODY _____

NUMBER _____

PLURAL NOUN _____

VERB _____

SILLY WORD_____

ADJECTIVE_____

NOUN _____

ADJECTIVE_____

SOMETHING ALIVE _____

PLURAL NOUN _____

MAD LIBS
TIME TO CELEBRATE!

The gang decided to throw a beach party on the shores of Madagascar. Gloria baked a huge _____ (NOUN) made of fresh _____ (SOMETHING ALIVE (PLURAL)) and whipped cream. It was really _____ (ADJECTIVE)! Melman was in charge of making sure that everyone had a/an _____ (ADJECTIVE) place to _____ (VERB). Marty and Alex decided to sing a duet, so they spent all day practicing songs like "Shake Your _____ (PART OF THE BODY)" by _____ (NUMBER) Degrees, "Fun in the Sun" by the Beach _____ (PLURAL NOUN), and "I Love to _____ (VERB)" by Lindsay _____ (SILLY WORD). The penguins were so excited about the party, they decided to do a/an _____ (ADJECTIVE) dance originally choreographed by the New York City _____ (NOUN)! The dance company was really _____ (ADJECTIVE). Afterward, they drank a toast with fresh juice made out of _____ (SOMETHING ALIVE). Cheers to the Madagascar _____ (PLURAL NOUN)!

From MADAGASCAR MAD LIBS®, Madagascar TM & © 2005 DreamWorks Animation L.L.C. Published by Price Stern Sloan, a division of Penguin Young Readers Group, 345 Hudson Street, New York, New York 10014.

This book is published by

PSS!

PRICE STERN SLOAN

whose other splendid titles include such literary classics as

The Original #1 Mad Libs®
Son of Mad Libs®
Sooper Dooper Mad Libs®
Monster Mad Libs®
Goofy Mad Libs®
Off-the-Wall Mad Libs®
Vacation Fun Mad Libs®
Camp Daze Mad Libs®
Christmas Fun Mad Libs®
Mad Libs® 40th Anniversary Deluxe Edition
Mad Mad Mad Mad Mad Libs®
Mad Libs® On the Road
Austin Powers™ Mad Libs®
The Powerpuff Girls™ Mad Libs®
Scooby-Doo!™ Mad Libs®
Scooby-Doo!™ Halloween Mad Libs®
Scooby-Doo!™ Mystery Mad Libs®
Scooby-Doo!™ Movie Mad Libs®
Scooby-Doo!™ 2 Monsters Unleashed Mad Libs®
Shrek™ Mad Libs®
Shrek 2™ Mad Libs®
Catwoman™ Mad Libs®
Fear Factor™ Mad Libs®
Fear Factor™ Mad Libs®: Ultimate Gross Out!
Survivor™ Mad Libs®
Guinness World Records™ Mad Libs®
The Mad Libs® Worst-Case Scenario™ Survival Handbook
The Mad Libs® Worst-Case Scenario™ Survival Handbook 2
The Mad Libs® Worst-Case Scenario Survival Handbook™: Travel
The Mad Libs® Worst-Case Scenario Survival Handbook™: Holidays
American Idol™ Mad Libs®
Teen Titans™ Mad Libs®
Graduation Mad Libs®

and many, many more!
Mad Libs® are available wherever books are sold.